Bantam Books in the Choose Your Own Adventure® series
Ask your bookseller for the books you have missed

CHOOSE YOUR OWN ADVENTURE® • 107

FIGHT FOR FREEDOM

BY JAY LEIBOLD

ILLUSTRATED BY LESLIE MORRILL

An R.A. Montgomery Book

BANTAM BOOKS
NEW YORK • TORONTO • LONDON • SYDNEY • AUCKLAND

All the characters in this book are fictitious. Any resemblance to persons living or dead is purely coincidental.

The author and publisher would like to thank Jerry Mofokeng and Cindy Ruskin for their assistance.

RL 4, age 10 and up

FIGHT FOR FREEDOM

A Bantam Book / November 1990

CHOOSE YOUR OWN ADVENTURE® *is a registered trademark of Bantam Books, a division of Bantam Doubleday Dell Publishing Group, Inc. Registered in U.S. Patent and Trademark Office and elsewhere.*

Original conception of Edward Packard

Cover art by George Tsui
Interior illustrations by Leslie Morrill

ISBN 0-553-28766-4

Published simultaneously in the United States and Canada

Bantam Books are published by Bantam Books, a division of Bantam Doubleday Dell Publishing Group, Inc. Its trademark, consisting of the words "Bantam Books" and the portrayal of a rooster, is Registered in U.S. Patent and Trademark Office and in other countries. Marca Registrada. Bantam Books, 666 Fifth Avenue, New York, New York 10103.

PRINTED IN THE UNITED STATES OF AMERICA

OPM   0 9 8 7 6 5 4 3 2 1

FIGHT FOR FREEDOM

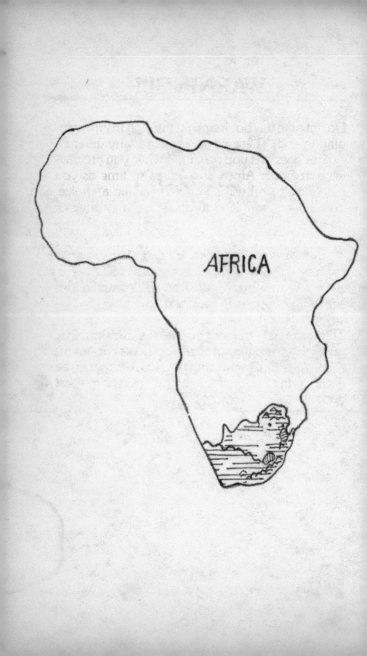

WARNING!!!

Do not read this book straight through from beginning to end. These pages contain many different experiences that you may have while you are traveling in South Africa. From time to time as you read along, you will be asked to make a choice. Your choice may lead to a successful journey or disaster.

The adventures you have are the results of your choices. You are responsible because you choose. After you make a choice, follow the instructions to see what happens to you next.

Think carefully before you make a decision. The government's policy of apartheid makes South Africa a tense and frightening place. Your trip may be exciting, but you might also find yourself in great danger.

Good luck!

HISTORICAL NOTE

The country known as South Africa was originally inhabited by a number of different African peoples. When European settlers arrived in the late seventeenth century they brought with them rigid classifications of race, which led to a belief in white supremacy. Dutch immigrants started farming the Cape of Good Hope area, intermixing with the people already there. These Dutch farmers, along with immigrants from other European countries, became known as Afrikaners, and developed their own language, Afrikaans.

Over time the Afrikaners, also known as Boers, made treks into the interior of the country, displacing Africans and taking away their land. They fought a series of wars with peoples such as the Zulus, and later with the English. By 1948 the Afrikaner-led Nationalist Party swept into power. This party, which has never lost an election since, instituted the current system of *apartheid*.

Apartheid is an essential tool used by the government to maintain white domination. The black population is five times larger than that of the white, yet apartheid gives the white minority a great deal of control over the black majority.

During the 1970s government laws not only segregated the races, they were in the process of taking South African citizenship away from blacks. Many blacks had been thrown out of their houses, and were confined to ghettolike "townships" and "settlements." Others had been moved to tribal "homelands," which were supposed to be ancestral territories. Yet these homelands make up only 13% of the country, with the best land saved for whites.

South Africa, with its diamonds, gold mines, and mineral resources, is one of the richest countries in the world, but the black population profits little from it. Many blacks have a poor standard of living or are unemployed. The average black worker receives one-tenth the wages of a white, and the best jobs are reserved—by law—for whites. Most blacks must travel a long way to find work, often leaving their families for eleven months out of the year.

For decades blacks have been demanding racial equality, full political rights, and educational and economic opportunities. One of the leading organizations in the fight against apartheid has been the African Nationalist Congress (A.N.C.). Its leader, Nelson Mandela, was imprisoned in 1964. In the 1950s he fought for nonviolent change, but after the South African police massacred demonstrators in Sharpeville in 1960, he turned to armed struggle. Explaining that he did so in self-defense, he said at his trial, "I have fought against white domination. I have fought against black domination. I have cherished the idea of a democratic and free society in which all persons live together in harmony, and with equal opportunities. . . . It is an ideal for which I am prepared to die."

Mandela stuck by his ideals, and was finally released from prison in February 1990. At the time of this writing, he and other black leaders are negotiating for an end to apartheid, and for meaningful political representation.

SPECIAL NOTE
TO THE READER

The action of this book takes place in South Africa in 1976. At that time the government showed little sign of changing its policy of apartheid. Blacks, especially black students, were showing their anger with increasing intensity.

In recent months there have been a number of changes. Nelson Mandela, leader of the African National Congress, has been released from prison, and most antiapartheid groups have been legalized. The white government appears willing to negotiate with black leaders.

The roots and effects of racism, however, run deep. Blacks in South Africa have endured three centuries of subjugation by European colonizers. Even if apartheid is eliminated and blacks gain basic civil rights and political power, healing and conciliation will be a long and difficult process. Conservative forces in the white community will not give up their privileges easily; other whites are fearful of black rage after centuries of injustice. Nevertheless, at present there is a great deal of hope.

The state-enforced racism depicted in this book may well be coming to an end. It is our hope that the future will bring freedom, justice, and equality for all of South Africa.

Your stomach tightens into a knot as you and your travel group approach the border. You've flown from the United States to Swaziland, and now you're crossing into South Africa. The year is 1976, and you are about to come face to face with apartheid—the South African government's policy of segregation and racial discrimination.

Joyce Jenkins, the leader of your group, suggested that you visit Swaziland first before entering South Africa. She thought it would be a good introduction to the continent.

Your day and a half in Mbabane, the capital, has been fascinating. There is more tourism and industry than you expected, and the people are easygoing and friendly. Now, approaching the South African border, you're struck by the contrast. Heavy concrete buildings and armed security police make you aware of the military and technological might of the white-ruled state. Even though you and your group have been invited as guests, you have an instinctive reaction to this bristling fortress.

The knot in your stomach clenches a little more as you enter the immigration office with Joyce. Inside, there are three windows. One is marked "Republic of South Africa Passports," where a few white men and women stand in line; another window is marked "Travel Documents," with a long line of blacks; and a third is marked "Foreign Passports."

Turn to page 2.

Joyce walks right up to the last window and presents her papers. The steely eyed immigration officer seems to register the color of her skin. He surveys the papers, then looks over the many people of color in your eight-member group. You try to read what is behind his eyes, but he merely presses his lips together and says, "Wait here."

As you wait for the officer to return, you think back to the events that have brought you here.

You're the editor of your school newspaper back in New York City, and Joyce is your adviser. Last fall, she encouraged you to enter a national essay contest on education. You decided to take on a difficult subject—education in South Africa. In the course of your research you learned about apartheid. You discovered that the South African government's system of forced racial segregation has created enormous inequalities.

Here black students are given a totally different kind of education than whites. White leaders have decided that blacks can be trained only for low-level labor and declared that blacks should have no hope of ever becoming equal with whites. One Prime Minister even said, "There is no place for the black student in the European community above the level of certain forms of labor."

Go on to the next page.

Not only are black students not allowed to attend the same schools as whites, but schools for blacks receive less money than white schools do. Yet blacks, who have less money, have to pay for their education; white students don't. The conclusion of your essay stated that the system of education under apartheid plays a crucial role in keeping blacks from getting good jobs and bettering their lives.

A couple of months later, you received a letter from Jack Lambert, a public relations man for a multinational corporation. He said he was impressed by your essay but that you should come to South Africa at his company's expense to see what they were doing to help change the situation. He hoped Joyce, as your adviser, would agree to be your sponsor and said you could bring along six other interested students.

You discussed the invitation with Joyce, who is active in the movement against apartheid. "It's a fascinating opportunity. But if we go," she warned, "we must be careful. They wouldn't have invited us unless they believed they could use our visit to their advantage. I'm sure we'll only be shown what they want us to see. We may think we'll be able to see things the way they really are, but it won't be so easy."

You decided to go ahead with the trip, organizing a group of students from your school who were concerned about South Africa.

Go on to the next page.

4

You also managed to get an assignment from a national scholastic magazine to write about your experiences on the trip. You left at the beginning of summer vacation, and after a brief stop in Swaziland, you are now about to spend a week in South Africa. Your visit will include a meeting with a minister in the Department of Education in Pretoria and end in Cape Town on the Atlantic coast.

You're nervous about venturing into a country where apartheid is the law of the land. Apartheid divides the people of South Africa into four races: those of African descent (blacks), those of European descent (whites), people of mixed race ("coloreds"), and people from India. Here in South Africa, people of different races aren't allowed to live in the same neighborhood. Blacks are not allowed to use the same restaurants, hotels, buses, trains, taxis, beaches, and scores of other services available to whites. Apartheid is just one of the methods used by white rulers to subjugate the "nonwhite" majority politically and economically.

Before you left you wondered if the authorities would segregate your group, most of whom are not white. "They make provisions for foreigners," Joyce said in answer to your question. "There are so-called international hotels and restaurants where anyone who can afford it can go. Foreign visitors are treated as 'honorary whites' and are allowed to enter 'white only' establishments."

"What a thrill," you remarked sarcastically.

Turn to page 58.

You have to admit, though, that the elementary school Mr. Vorman takes you to doesn't look so bad. Granted it's nothing more than a concrete box on the barren, dusty outskirts of a village, but the students do have pencils, paper, and books. Most of them are neatly dressed, though when you look closely you see that their clothes are either too big or too small because they are well patched hand-me-downs.

You know from your essay research that even a school of this quality is one in a thousand. Where schools do exist for blacks, they are overcrowded, poorly equipped, and short on teachers, books, and, most of all, any real learning.

After your tour of the school, Joyce asks your guide, "Mr. Vorman, do you suppose we could have a couple of hours to wander around the village on our own?"

"Oh, that's not a very good idea, Ms. Jenkins," he says, pulling at his mustache. "There are *skollies*—bandits—in these parts."

"That's often true of economically deprived areas," Joyce replies coolly. "But I'm sure we can look out for ourselves."

Vorman reluctantly agrees. Tapping his watch, he says, "Don't forget, we have to leave for the train station in two hours for your meeting in Pretoria with Jack Lambert and the Deputy Minister."

"We'll be there," Joyce says. "Thank you." Turning to the group, she announces, "Everyone stay together. If we get separated, meet back here in the parking lot. We can't miss that train!"

Turn to page 60.

The bus doesn't pull into a "closer settlement" depot until one in the morning. "Last stop!" the driver announces. You despair of reaching Johannesburg in time to catch Willem and his gang.

The depot is nothing more than a fenced-off clearing in the bush outside the settlement. You slump down against a bench and close your eyes. If it wasn't for a cold wind blowing through your thin coat, you'd try to get some sleep.

Two hours later you're surprised when passengers arrive to wait for the bus. Many of them are carrying lunch bags or pails. You approach one woman and ask, "Are you on the night shift?"

She looks at you as if you are crazy. "My job starts at seven o'clock," she replies.

"You must be going a long way."

"Just to Johannesburg, like everyone else," she shrugs. "Most of us work for ten hours, then try to get back home by eight at night."

You hear the sound of a diesel engine, and the bus comes roaring up, its lights illuminating the sleepy group of commuters. "Late again," the woman says as you follow her on board.

Once the passengers get settled, they immediately fall asleep. Some put small cushions on the back of the seat in front of them, lean their foreheads on the cushion, and doze off. Others slump against the person next to them. Later, as the bus fills up, some of the commuters fold themselves up and sleep in pretzellike positions on the floor. The bus bounces over rough roads. Dim green interior lights cast an eerie glow over the scene.

Turn to page 59.

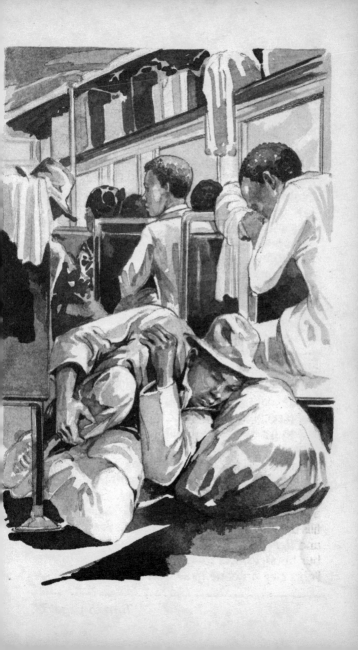

Five minutes later, your plan set, you march up the driveway. You have no idea if this will work. You'll just have to go on nerve, you think, as you burst through the door.

The four men inside stare at you in shock. One of them quickly pulls his gun on you. "Don't make a move," he says. You recognize the voice as Hendrik's. Under his close-cut blond hair you can see scars on his skull.

Somehow you maintain a facade of calm. "I'm not worried," you say. "The police are only a couple of minutes behind me."

"Maybe we'll kill you just for the fun of it," Hendrik snarls.

"You haven't committed murder—yet," you reply. "But if you want that pinned on you along with terrorism and conspiracy, go ahead. I'm willing to die for the cause."

"And so am I," Hendrik says, cocking his gun. He doesn't bother asking you what cause you mean—he assumes you're with black freedom fighters, like the A.N.C.

"Hold on a second, Hendrik," Willem says. "We'll want to get some information out of this one." He turns to you with a malicious grin. "Surely you're not so stupid as to think you can threaten us with the police. They won't help you. They're on *our* side."

Turn to page 65.

You draw on the research you did for your essay to point out that this is not a fact of nature, but the result of colonial domination and lack of opportunity. You argue that the government has withheld proper education from blacks so that they'll continue to provide cheap labor and won't be able to compete with whites for jobs.

Johannes bristles a little as he thumps his chest and says, "Look at me. I didn't go much for school. I learned what I needed to know from the land, from my ancestors."

"Yes," you reply, "but you've had advantages that no black is given." Then, remembering that you need him to help you, you add, "Of course, I don't mean to take anything away from your accomplishments. You have a beautiful farm."

You thank Evelyn when the meal is over and ask Johannes if he could take you to the nearest bus stop. You explain that you're sure you can get a job if only you can make it to Johannesburg.

"I'll have to admit, you sound pretty intelligent for a—well, you know." He thinks for a moment, then shrugs. "Sure, I can give you a ride."

Turn to page 57.

Fascinated, you walk over to the window and peer inside, amazed by what you see. The room is lit by candles, which cast a flickering light on the mysterious objects on the walls and floor—bones, roots, leaves, and various kinds of bottles, as well as dead frogs, snakes, and even a human skull.

A man and boy are kneeling before an incredible figure—the one you caught a glimpse of before. The figure, his face set in a stern expression, is plastered with red clay. He is robed in fur, bones, shells, and gourds. He waves a stick over the two of them, murmuring incantations.

You're so mesmerized by the sight that you're unaware of the young woman looking over your shoulder. She's about your age, and you give a start when you notice her. "I'm sorry," you stammer. "I was just—"

"It's okay," she says in accented English. "I don't see *sangomas* very often, either."

"You mean a witch doctor?" you ask. "What's he doing to the man and boy?"

The girl shrugs. "He could be helping the man get a job, or pay his rent, or be safe from the police. Or maybe he's curing the boy of an illness, or helping him do well in school."

"Oh," you say, a little disappointed. You imagined witch doctors casting more exotic spells.

Suddenly you realize you should take notes. You get a pad out of your backpack and say, "I'm writing a story for an American magazine. Can I ask you some questions?"

"Sure," the girl says.

Turn to page 67.

12

You soon come face to face with the demonstration. Roger is driving down a street when suddenly, coming the other way, you see a mass of marching students. Roger quickly pulls off to park on a side street. Once again, he stays in the car while you get out to see what's going on.

The approaching demonstration is an impressive sight. Thousands of students wave banners and punch their fists in the air chanting, *"Amandla! Awethu!"*—"Power is ours!" You watch for a minute, awestruck, before you remember you have to locate Abraham Mabaso.

Suddenly a wave of confusion spreads through the crowd. People start running and shouting angrily. From what you can make out, the cause is a report that the police have shot and killed several small children in another part of the township.

Turn to page 49.

You plop down by the side of the road in complete desolation. A sense of panic wells up inside you. You've never felt so isolated and so alone before. You can't really blame Joyce and the group for leaving—they had to be sure and make it to their meeting with the minister in the Department of Education. You must get a grip on yourself, though. There has to be a way for you to get to the train station, and from there on to Pretoria.

But suddenly a new thought occurs to you. Maybe this is not such a disaster after all, but an opportunity. Maybe this is your chance to see the real South Africa—to wander around on your own for a few days and really experience the country. If what Jack Lambert and the minister have to say are anything like Mr. Vorman's canned speech, you won't be missing out on much there. A whole new world of possibility opens up for you. Imagine what the editors of the magazine would say if they saw a story like this!

On the other hand, perhaps the idea is a foolish one. It may be difficult—not to mention dangerous—for you to travel alone. With the school protests going on in Soweto, there's a lot of tension throughout the country. The police are taking repressive measures. There may be something to be said for playing it safe and trying to get to Pretoria as soon as possible.

If you decide you'd better try to get to Pretoria, turn to page 104.

If you decide to travel on your own, turn to page 74.

The minister interrupts you to ask if you'd like some tea. You nod, and as soon as he returns with a pot of hot rooibos tea, you resume your story. You notice that Roger serves you with the same kind of teacup that he is using—many whites in South Africa have separate dishes for blacks.

When you are finished, Roger pulls at his collar. "My, this is terrible. We must do something."

"Exactly," you say. "Obviously we can't go to the police."

"Yes, hmm, my my," he murmurs, rubbing his fleshy chin. You know, I'm a very strong opponent of apartheid. But I don't usually come up against this sort of . . ." He consults his watch. "It's just about my bedtime. From the look of you, you could use some rest, too. Why don't we sleep on it?"

"But by then it'll be too late to do anything," you protest.

"Oh, no, I get up well before dawn," Roger answers with a smile. "We'll have time then to decide what to do."

Turn to page 21.

You find Mbuto's distant kinsmen living on top of the second hill, next to a *kraal,* in a round mud hut with a thatched roof. They welcome their long-lost "cousin" with open arms and prepare an enormous feast for the two of you.

The next day the grandfather of the family takes you into a nearby town and arranges for you to stow away in the back of a bakery truck making its weekly rounds from Johannesburg. Before he leaves you off, he presses some money into Mbuto's hand.

The truck is perfect for you and Mbuto since you're on the run. Hidden away behind empty bread shelves, you're able to avoid roadblocks.

"Where does Soweto get its name?" you ask during your ride.

"It's from southwestern township," Mbuto explains. "Thirty years ago, black people were able to live in Johannesburg like anyone else. Then the government began its system of segregation, forcing people out of their homes and into cement boxes they'd built over the ridge from Johannesburg. Yet every morning the residents still have to jam onto the buses and trains to go to work in Johannesburg. Most people have no electricity, not to mention running water, telephones, or toilets. No privacy either, for that matter, because the houses are so small and crowded."

Go on to the next page.

"I hear it's a dangerous place—there are lots of gangs and violence," you say.

"That's very true," Mbuto replies. "It tends to happen when people have their homes, their rights, and their dignity taken away from them. But still, the homelands are so barren that people go to great lengths to migrate to Soweto."

Turn to page 89.

There are only three rooms in the house, and the furnishings are bare—a single oilcloth-covered table, rickety chairs, and wooden crates. There's no electricity, and water must be carried from a spring half a kilometer away. Her family, it appears, saves everything—plastic bags, jars, squares of cloth—as if they were treasures.

When you walk in, six or seven children of varying ages are dancing to African pop music playing on a transistor radio. An elderly woman, who appears to be an invalid, sits bundled up in the corner. Mary engages in lively and affectionate banter with her younger siblings as she lights up a kerosene stove to start the evening meal.

Turn to page 27.

The first thing you're aware of when you return to consciousness is a tremendous pounding in your head. You are in total darkness, in a cramped space, unable to move because you are bound and gagged. Once you smell exhaust fumes and feel the vibrations, you realize that you are in the trunk of a car. Not only that, but your backpack containing your money and passport is gone.

A while later the car pulls over. You pretend to be unconscious as the trunk is opened and you are unceremoniously lifted out and dumped on the ground like a sack of potatoes. You wait for the car to drive off before you struggle to your feet.

Once your eyes adjust to the darkness, you realize you are in the open, rolling countryside. It must be the veld—the huge region of high grassland which covers much of the interior of South Africa.

A small cluster of lights twinkle in the distance. Despite the ropes on your arms and legs, you find you are able to move forward by making little hops. You start across the veld toward the lights.

Suddenly you find yourself tripping over the edge of a small gully and sliding all the way to the bottom. Luckily it is dry. In order to get back up the other side, you must wriggle on your knees and elbows like a worm. By the time you get there you're soaked with sweat.

You lie on your back panting for a few minutes, staring up at the unfamiliar stars of the Southern Hemisphere. At this rate, you think, it'll take forever to reach the lights.

Turn to page 94.

You nod numbly. Suddenly you do feel exhausted. You allow Roger to lead you to a guest room, but you can't fall asleep. You toss and turn, growing itchy for action. Time is slipping away. You fear that however benevolent Roger's intentions are, it may be beyond him to actually *do* something. Unless—maybe what he needs is to be pushed a little. Maybe you should go wake him up and tell him to get moving right away.

Your only other option is to sneak out of his house and go it on your own.

*If you decide to slip out of the house,
turn to page 62.*

*If you decide to wake Roger up,
turn to page 78.*

You pick out four voices as the men talk. At first their accents sound strange, then you realize they are Afrikaners. They seem to be laying out a plan. As you listen, you gradually realize that the object of their plan is to set off a bomb!

"We know he'll be in Soweto," the man named Willem says. "The only question is where. Hendrik and I will go to Johannesburg tonight and meet with our government friends. They should have the information from their informers. Stephan, you and Osgood stay here and finish the bomb. We'll all meet in Johannesburg tomorrow morning at ten o'clock. You have the address?"

"34 Verhoeven, right?"

"That's it. How's the bomb coming along?"

"I've got everything I need," Stephan replies. "I can finish it tonight. It'll take him out all right—not to mention his bodyguards and half the neighborhood."

"The more we kill, the less money we have to spend on their lousy homelands," a nasty voice says.

Go on to the next page.

"Not to mention education," Stephan puts in. "This bomb will give them something to worry about other than complaining about having to use Afrikaans in school. If they want to live in our country, then they should use the language."

"That's not what the European settlers said about African languages when they arrived here," you silently reply to Stephan.

"The main thing, Hendrik, is to get Abraham Mabaso out of the way," Willem says.

You can't believe your ears. Abraham Mabaso is a leader of the movement against apartheid!

"We'll teach him a lesson," Hendrik snarls. "We'll teach all those *kaffirs* to stay in their place."

"You'll make the bomb as we discussed, Stephan?" Willem says.

"It'll look like it came straight from the Soviets."

"Excellent," Willem says. "Not only will we get Mabaso out of the way, the A.N.C. will get the blame. The blacks will start fighting among themselves, and our white brothers will have second thoughts about any talk of reform."

"And the brotherhood will rule!" Hendrik cries.

Turn to page 86.

The group of you are hauled down to the police station as if you were criminals. "You can't treat me like this!" you say. "I'm an American. I can prove it!"

The officer in charge holds out his hand for your papers. You reach for your backpack—and then realize it's not on you. "I left it in the car," you say with irritation, turning to walk out. "I'll go get it."

A guard quickly grabs you. "You're not going anywhere but into the maximum security cell," the officer barks.

You're dragged down a long corridor and sent sprawling onto the floor. "You'll be sorry!" you scream at the guard as he closes the bars.

Then you notice a man quietly sitting in the corner, his knees drawn up. "Why will they be sorry?" he asks calmly.

"None of your business," you snap. Later, though, when you've calmed down, you start to talk to your cellmate. His name is Mbuto, and he has an air of confidence and resolve that makes you feel you can trust him. He seems intrigued by the fact that you came to South Africa to report on apartheid. He wants to hear all about New York and life in the United States.

"I don't understand these policemen," you say, gesturing at your cell bars. "I'd think the black police in the homelands would be better."

Mbuto shakes his head. "Sometimes they are the worst," he says sadly. "It's almost as if they have to prove their loyalty to their white bosses."

"But why do they do it? Why do they join the repressive regime?"

Turn to page 108.

You're up early in the morning to have breakfast with Jack Lambert. Then you're whisked off for your meeting with the minister in the Department of Education.

Although your group has only half an hour with the minister, for you it is a depressing thirty minutes. He's a hard-line conservative and gives no ground on any of the issues you bring up. Your meeting inspires little hope for change.

When you ask pointed questions about his new policy of making black students study in Afrikaans, he becomes very abrupt. "Afrikaans is one of the official languages of this country. If these students don't want to learn it, they should go back to their tribal homelands."

"But they already have to learn English," you say. "Afrikaans is of little use to them in dealing with the rest of the world. It limits their education."

"Our Africans have little need to deal with the outside world," responds the minister. Checking his watch, he says, "It's thirty-five past the hour. I'm afraid this meeting has gone overtime."

As he shows you to the door, you can't resist the opportunity to tell him he ought to work on his diplomacy skills. Joyce hurries you out of the office before you get yourself in trouble.

When you get down to the lobby, Lambert says to your group, "I must confess, I'm embarrassed by our minister. Many of us who are working for reform in this country regard his attitudes as backward. At least by meeting him, you have an idea of what we're up against."

Turn to page 92.

"When are your parents coming home?" you ask one of the kids.

"Maybe at Christmas," she replies shyly.

You look at Mary, who explains, "My mother and father work in Johannesburg. Father is a mechanic, and mother works as a nanny for a white family. The government won't let us move there with them. My grandmother is sick, so it's up to me to raise the children here." Seeing the surprised look on your face, she adds, "We do see our parents for one month out of the year, usually in December."

"Isn't it kind of strange that your mother spends all of her time looking after someone else's children, and yet because of the laws, she cannot care for her own?" you ask.

Mary just nods and looks down at the floor.

As you settle down to a dinner of corn porridge, the staple of the diet, with a little pork fat and wild greens added, Mary tells you that her parents are actually fortunate. "At least they get to see each other in Johannesburg once in a while. Many men in the village work as gold miners. The work is backbreaking, and they must live in crowded single-sex hostels, where no outsiders are allowed."

Turn to page 102.

You agree to try Henry's plan. First it's a two-hour walk to the railroad tracks. Then you sneak into the railyard through a gap in the fence. You settle down behind some rusted metal drums and wait.

It's almost dark out by the time you hear the whistle of an approaching freight train. Once it stops, Henry leads you out to the boxcars. To your relief, one of them is empty and the doors are open, so you don't have to ride on the roof.

Henry helps you inside. The whistle blows again, and the engines chuff out of the yard.

The train pulls into Pretoria a few hours before dawn. Stiff and chilled, you and Henry climb out. You dodge in among the railway cars, managing to keep away from the security patrols. In a remote part of the railyard, you find a group of black men huddled around a fire. You crouch down by the fire while Henry talks to the men.

"Nobody here knows when the next train leaves for Johannesburg," Henry says when he returns. "Maybe we should continue on another way. The railyard police are very sharp around here."

You have a sudden thought. "Maybe we don't need to go to Johannesburg," you say. "My travel group is meeting here in Pretoria with a minister in the Department of Education today. We could try to find them . . . but wait a minute, it'll never work. Without the right papers, they'll never let us inside."

Henry furrows his brow. "That's no problem," he says. "I can get us in." He beckons you to follow him.

Turn to page 84.

You and Henry grab a couple of brooms and push them all the way over to the office of the minister. You push right past a protesting secretary and burst into the minister's chambers. You're glad to see that Joyce and your group, along with a man in a business suit, are seated around a table with the minister.

"What's the meaning of this?" the minister demands, outraged. "Can't you see I have guests? I will not be interrupted by two—two—"

"You've got to act quickly," you say. "There's a plot to set off a bomb in Soweto. I know where the plotters are meeting in Johannesburg in one hour. There's still time to catch them."

While the minister continues to glare at you, your name suddenly bursts from Joyce's lips. "Why didn't you tell us it was you?" she says, running over to give you a big hug. "Where have you been?"

Turn to page 36.

You clamber up on top of the bales of hay and crawl to the front of the truck, holding on to the wires that bind the bales in order to keep your balance. You turn around and start pounding on the roof of the cab with your feet.

The farmer pulls over into the parking lot of the restaurant to see what's going on. But when he slams on the brakes you go tumbling head over heels, bouncing off the hood of the truck before landing on the pavement.

The farmer jumps out and rushes to your side. "Hey, are you all right?" he asks.

"I think so," you say, somewhat shaken.

After you've brushed yourself off and decided you're in one piece, the farmer starts to get mad. "What the devil were you doing on top of my truck, anyway? I didn't give you permission to ride with me. You could have been killed!"

"It's a long story," you say quickly, holding up your arms to protect yourself. "Please forgive me. It won't happen again."

The farmer eyes you, his hands on his hips. Knowing that his reaction could have been a lot more violent, you decide not to press your luck. "I think I'll just pop in for a bite to eat," you say casually, heading toward the restaurant.

"Good luck," he calls, throwing up his arms.

You wonder why his voice has an ironic bite to it. Then you notice a sign in the window of the restaurant. In Afrikaans, it says, NET BLANKES, but you can guess its meaning: WHITES ONLY.

Turn to page 96.

You grab the bomb and bolt for the front door, only to find it blocked by a snarling German shepherd. "Back door!" you shout to Roger.

He turns and takes two steps before colliding headlong with the first of the men coming down the stairs. You crash into the second one, and all four of you go sprawling to the floor.

Luckily, you and Roger are more awake than the men are. You get back on your feet quickly, pick up the bomb, and dash for the back door. Roger is right behind you.

As you stop to unlock the door, Roger grabs your arm. "What's ticking?"

You look down at the device cradled against your chest. You've armed the bomb!

You drop it and fumble frantically with the lock. Roger kicks the bomb back into the hallway. Finally you jerk the door open and the two of you stumble outside. Moments later a tremendous blast throws you to the ground.

You and Roger pick yourself up from under the debris. Shakily you check yourselves out, relieved to find you've escaped with only minor cuts and bruises.

The first officer to arrive on the scene is a highway patrolman. He jumps out of his car, gun drawn. "What's going on here?" he demands, as you dab the wound on your face.

Roger comes up from behind you, adjusting his collar. He draws himself up to his full stature. "Watch your tone," he warns the officer. "You're talking to a hero."

The End

You direct the driver of your land rover out of the village and through the bush on a faint dirt track. As you draw closer to a ravine covered with thicker growth, you lean forward and tap the captain on the shoulder, saying, "It's down there."

The vehicles skid to a halt. The captain jumps out and pulls Mbuto from his seat. "Where is it?" he demands. Mbuto just stares at him. The captain cuffs him on the ear, and Mbuto says a single word in an African language. Enraged, the captain pushes him into the ravine.

The captain and the two guards go running and sliding down the slope after him. But the moment they arrive, five black men emerge from the bushes. As the men battle in the bottom of the ravine, the two drivers draw their pistols and run to the edge. You charge up from behind and throw yourself into them as hard as you can. The three of you go rolling down the dusty slope.

You regain your feet first and scramble back up to the top, picking up a fallen pistol on the way. You jump into one of the land rovers and start the engine. A minute later Mbuto, covered with dust and blood, is beside you. "Let's go!" he cries.

You throw the gearshift into first and step on the gas. The engine just revs. "Let out the clutch!" Mbuto screams. You lift your left foot and the vehicle lurches violently into gear.

Once you've pulled away, Mbuto has you stop and use the pistol to shoot apart his handcuffs. You're nervous pulling the trigger, but it works. You trade seats and roar off through the bush.

Turn to page 105.

"In 1960 everything changed when the police massacred 69 protestors in Sharpeville," Mbuto continues. "We realized nonviolence was getting us nowhere. The regime was waging undeclared war on blacks, and it was self-defense to fight back. People who have as much wealth and privilege as the whites do are not going to hand it over if you simply say 'please.' You have to be able to back up your demands."

"Was that when the A.N.C. formed a military wing?" you ask.

"That's right," Mbuto responds. "And it didn't take long for the government to crack down on us. They outlawed political organizations and sent the leaders into jail. Some were exiled."

"Nelson Mandela is still in prison," you note.

"Exactly," Mbuto says. "That's the real crime." He lowers his voice. "Let me tell you something. Not so long ago, I was a lawyer. I had a decent house, an automobile, a family. I tried to fight apartheid through the system. Then one night the security police came for me. I was given no trial and allowed no communication with my family. I won't tell you what they did to me in detention.

"Then one day they let me go," Mbuto continues, "but they told me I was banned. That meant I had to resign from my job, I couldn't meet with more than one person at a time, I couldn't publish—I couldn't do anything. I was a nonperson. For me, that was the end. I slipped away from my police watchdogs and went over the border to join the A.N.C. in exile."

Turn to page 114.

"I'll tell you later," you say. "Right now we've got to stop this plot. We need to call the Johannesburg police *now*."

The minister is still skeptical. "I need more evidence than this. With all due respect, I can't act on a rumor from some, er . . ."

The man in the business suit seizes the opportunity to speak up. "You were the one just talking about mutual respect. Show us a sign of your good faith. Call the police."

"All right," the minister agrees reluctantly. "I'll send a squad of police to check out that address."

An hour later, a return call comes: the right-wing extremists have been caught in the act. The minister looks at you and Henry with a mixture of sheepishness and resentment. "I guess I owe you two an apology," he says.

The End

You're not exactly sure how you're going to stop the bomb plot by yourself, but one thing is certain—the assassins are getting away fast. You circle in back of some outbuildings behind the house and come out just in time to see Willem's car going up a long dirt driveway leading to the main road.

You take a deep breath and burst into a run through the cornfield. The plume of dust behind their car helps obscure the sight of you. Coming out of the cornfield, you notice a farmer's truck loaded with hay approaching an intersection off to the right.

Willem's car reaches the main road and, without stopping, turns left. The hay truck also has its left-turn signal on. You put some extra kick into your run to intercept the truck.

By the time you get to the road, the farmer has made his turn. You try to wave at him, but he's already past you. As the truck accelerates, you make one final sprint. At the last moment you grab the back and pull yourself onto the flatbed.

Turn to page 112.

"Those men are terrorists!" you cry, pointing your finger at Willem and Hendrik. Now you've got everybody's attention. "They're planning to murder Abraham Mabaso. I heard it with my own ears. Somebody help me stop them!"

Pandemonium breaks out in the restaurant. Some of the patrons start moving toward Willem and Hendrik's table. Others cheer them on with words of praise. Scuffles break out.

Hendrik quickly puts a stop to it all when he draws a pistol and fires it into the ceiling. Everyone freezes. You have a pretty clear idea who's in control of the situation now—the one with the gun. It takes about a millisecond for you to realize you are in great danger. You quickly bolt out the door.

You come into the parking lot just in time to see the hay truck still there, pulling away. A burst of speed, fueled by fear, allows you to catch up with it. Again you grab onto the back and jump aboard. The farmer will certainly be surprised to see you again.

It seems to take him a painfully long time to shift the truck into a higher gear. As the gears grind, you see Willem and Hendrik jumping into their car. Soon they are on your tail. A bullet goes whizzing by your head. You dive behind a bale of hay. Bullets thunk into it.

Suddenly you have a brilliant idea. Maybe you're strong enough to push the bale of hay off the truck and into the path of Willem's car.

Turn to page 107.

Soon the helicopter lands, and you and Mbuto are taken into custody. The policemen handcuff you roughly and push you into the chopper. "No more homeland prison for you two," he says. "You're going to Pretoria."

As you fly to Pretoria, Mbuto whispers to you, "Tell them you're an American and act like we don't know each other. Try to get them to let you contact your group. Don't worry about me."

You shudder to think what will happen to Mbuto, but you realize he's right—you can do the most good by trying to get yourself released. As soon as you arrive at the huge concrete prison in Pretoria, you ask to see a police official.

"You'll get to see plenty of policemen," your guard says. "And you'll get to tell them everything you know."

"You don't understand," you say. "I'm an American."

Unfortunately, your pleas are of no use. You lost your backpack during the chase, and nothing you say convinces the police interrogators of your innocence. Not only that, you know that under the South African detention laws, you can be held without trial, and the police are not required to inform anyone of your whereabouts.

What's worse, you know that many prisoners have died "accidentally" in South African government prisons—from things like slipping on a bar of soap to falling out a window or committing suicide. You can only hope that your fate at the hands of the police will be different.

The End

The two of you flag down a passing car and get a ride to the farmer's house, which is just up the road. The driver leaves you off and promises to report the accident to the police for you.

"Johannes!" the farmer's wife cries when she opens the door. She brings the two of you inside and tends to your wounds. After you're both bandaged up, you look over at Johannes and say, "I'm sorry about all of this."

Johannes waves his hand. "Agh, don't worry about it. We Boers are a tough bunch!"

Now that you have the chance, you explain the bomb plot and the sequence of events leading up to the fiery crash on the highway. When you're finished, Johannes stares at you slack-jawed. You have no idea what he will say.

Slowly he shakes his head. "I have to tell you, you've been nothing but trouble from the moment I met you," he says. "It sounds to me like you're one of those foreigners trying to meddle in places where you don't belong. You don't understand our country. We have a good system here. The blacks here aren't civilized like you Americans. Apartheid is the only way to keep them under control." You can't believe what you're hearing, but you hold your tongue.

Turn to page 54.

You're awakened by footsteps on the porch. You jump up in panic, your mind a momentary blank. Then, as you hear angry voices, it all comes flooding back to you. Quickly you take cover in a closet as footsteps come clomping up the stairs. You scrunch yourself into a corner under some musty old drapes as someone enters the room. He gives a cursory look into the closet, then leaves.

Once the beating of your heart has calmed down and your breathing returns to normal, you can hear the men downstairs talking. "Everything is still here, Willem. The place is empty. It was probably just some poachers looking for food. We've got more important things to worry about."

"All right," Willem says. "I don't like it, but we don't have time to waste. Get out the maps."

You hear the men move into the living room and start murmuring among themselves. Creeping out of the closet to the top of the stairs, you eavesdrop on their conversation.

Turn to page 22.

42

"Staffriding sounds too dangerous," you say to Henry. "Let's get to the city some other way."

Henry goes along with you, but travel turns out to be very difficult. By the early morning hours, before dawn, you manage to make it to one of the "closer settlements" set aside for blacks near Pretoria.

You and Henry are walking through the darkened streets, trying to find someone who will loan you money to take a bus into Pretoria, when suddenly the streets come alive with half-clothed people fleeing in the opposite direction. Children are wailing and adults are yelling to one another, but you don't understand their urgent warnings. Henry stops a mother running away with her infant child to ask what's going on.

"Pass raid!" the woman gasps. You remember that this is when the police suddenly invade a neighborhood, trying to catch people whose passbooks aren't in order.

Before you can react, you're surrounded by policemen with bright flashlights and growling dogs. One of them slams Henry up against the fence. "Papers!" he demands.

Turn to page 55.

You decide to leave now, while you have the chance. As you head for the door, the two big Boers muscle up on either side of you. They ask the waitress if you're giving her trouble and if she wants you disposed of. "Please," she says acidly.

You're picked up by the scruff of your neck, legs dangling in the air, and unceremoniously heaved out the back door. You slide facedown in a puddle of greasy muck. The door slams behind you.

Peering up, you see a black man come out from behind a trash dumpster. He looks down at you sympathetically. "This is *our* dining room," he chuckles. You find it hard to laugh as you wipe the muck from your face.

The man hands you a drumstick and a discarded piece of bread. Suddenly you realize how hungry you are.

As you devour the food, the man tells you his name is Henry. He's a migrant worker. "I had land once," Henry says. "My family farmed it for generations. We had many cattle, and were respected by everyone in the community. But then the government came and threw me off our land. They told me I was on 'white land.' They moved me and my family to a 'group area' where they said the rest of my tribe was. But I didn't know any of those people.

"The land in the 'group area' is barren," Henry continues, "so now I must travel far from my home to find work. And the government won't even let me bring my family with me."

Turn to page 72.

You get out and manage to find someone who knows where Abraham Mabaso lives. A few hours later, exhausted, you finally find Abraham Mabaso's house and knock on the door. It opens a crack and a woman peeks out. "He's out on business," she says when you ask for him.

You realize she can't give any more information to a stranger. You take a guess where he might be. "Can you tell me where the demonstration is taking place?"

The woman gives you directions, and you trudge back to the car. "We have to go back across town," you tell Roger, who looks dismayed.

Turn to page 12.

Frikkie holds out his hand. "Passbook," he snaps.

"I don't need one," you say defiantly.

The sergeant arches his eyebrows. He gets up and walks in a slow circle around you, hands behind his back, inspecting you like a piece of merchandise. "Cheeky, aren't you?" he says. You grip the bottom of your seat to contain yourself.

"Hmmmm," he mumbles to himself, then gestures to his colleagues. "We may not have a pure-blooded Bantu here. What do you think, fellows?"

The policemen murmur in assent. "It takes a sharp eye to see these things," the sergeant goes on. "I'm no expert, but after a few years in this business, one learns how to make distinctions." He turns to you. "If I am mistaken, my deepest apologies. After all, if you're not black, we can't hold you. Tell us the truth, now: are you a colored, or a black?"

You grit your teeth to keep your anger under control. If you were South African, technically you would be considered "colored," since your parents are of different races.

Go on to the next page.

While blacks must carry a passbook at all times, "coloreds" do not. In all likelihood, if you tell Frikkie that you're colored, he will let you go. Coloreds receive slightly better treatment because they have "white blood" in them.

But everything in you resists going along with the sergeant's system and answering him. You hate the thought of caving in to his racial categories. Yet your release may depend on it.

If you swallow your pride and answer the sergeant's question, turn to page 73.

If you defy him and refuse to answer, turn to page 77.

Now a different feeling is in the air—you sense rage all around you. You smell smoke and then hear breaking glass. You look back at Roger. A large group of youths apparently have taken exception to his presence and are rocking his car back and forth. His back window is smashed.

Suddenly you hear the word *Mabaso*. As you turn, you hear the rev of an engine, then Roger's car peeling out. Meanwhile someone pushes you, and Abraham Mabaso is suddenly in front of you, being jostled in the crowd.

"Someone's plotting to assassinate you!" you call to him. "They're planning to set off a bomb this afternoon. You've got to get out of Soweto!"

Mabaso nods in acknowledgment, then he is swept off in the confusion. You make your way back to where you left Roger, but he's long gone. You hope you'll be able to get out of Soweto, and join up with Joyce and the group.

The End

You hold tight in your spot among the hay bales as the truck speeds by the restaurant. The next time you see Willem and Hendrik will be in Johannesburg, you hope.

A little way down the road, the farmer turns onto a long, dusty driveway and comes up to a cozy house set among eucalyptus trees. As he gets out of the cab, you jump down from the flatbed, picking pieces of hay from your clothes.

He jumps back in fright. "What the—"

"I hope you don't mind that I hitched a ride."

The farmer narrows his eyes, sizing you up. "Listen, I don't like stowaways. I ought to take you to the police. Do you have permission to be in this area? Where's your *baas?*"

"I don't have a boss," you begin nervously, getting ready to ward off a blow.

"Well I'm sorry, but I don't have any work. You understand?" He gives you a hard stare, then suddenly softens. "You have a strange accent. Where are you from?"

Go on to the next page.

You think quickly. If you tell him about the bomb plot, he might insist on taking you to the police, and you've already decided not to do that. Instead, you explain that you're a traveler from abroad, you've had your money and passport stolen, and you need to get to Johannesburg to find a job. "Please," you finish, "I need your help."

The farmer heaves his brawny shoulders in a sigh. His face is sunburned and weather-beaten, his hands thick and callused. You think he must be a Boer, an Afrikaner farmer. "*All* of you come to me for help," he mutters, motioning for you to follow him into the house.

Turn to page 90.

When Jack Lambert comes to pick you up the next morning, his face is drawn. He is worried that the whole country will be engulfed in violence. "I never thought it would come to this," he confesses.

"How could it *not* come to this?" Joyce says. "Whites have kept blacks down for way too long. There's no sign of change on the horizon. In fact, the government is just digging in its heels."

"Someday change will come," Lambert assures her. "I think the biggest problem is that whites are afraid. They're afraid of the kind of revenge blacks will want for all the years . . ."

"The longer you wait, though," someone from your group points out, "the worse the anger grows."

"And the harder it is to change," you add.

"True," Lambert says. "But you have to remember, in spite of what some people say, this *is* a democracy. The government can only move as fast as the voters allow it."

"The white voters, at any rate," you say.

"What about leadership?" Joyce asks. "That's what leaders are for—to help people see beyond their own limits."

"But don't you think whites have reason to be scared?" Lambert responds. "Look at Soweto today. Where are the black leaders?"

Go on to the next page.

"In prison and in exile," you reply. "Nelson Mandela is in jail, and the government has systematically crippled and outlawed organizations like the African National Congress. I don't believe the government wants black people to have real leaders."

"Look at how the security forces are trying to muzzle Steven Biko and the Black Consciousness movement," Joyce says. "If you keep eliminating the leadership, instead of having an organized opposition to negotiate with, of course you'll have anarchy and violence."

Turn to page 80.

Johannes pauses, then continues, "All the same, I don't believe in going around setting off bombs and assassinating people. That's just plain wrong." He raises himself from his bed with a groan. "Evelyn," he calls to his wife, "bring me the keys to the station wagon, and pack us some sandwiches. We're going to police headquarters in Johannesburg."

Half an hour later, you're on the way to Johannesburg in the backseat of Johannes and Evelyn's station wagon. You go straight to a police station, where Johannes reports all the information you've given him.

By the next afternoon, Stephan and Osgood have been nabbed red-handed with the bomb. You and Johannes are heroes, although Johannes is reluctant to be associated with the news. As for yourself, you'll have an exciting story to write when you get back home.

The End

Since neither you nor Henry have your papers in order, you're handcuffed together with a large group of blacks and hauled into a detention center. The next day you're brought before a magistrate who gives you 30 seconds to defend yourself. You begin to tell him you're visiting from the United States, when he slams his gavel and pronounces you guilty. You don't even get to the part about the bomb plot. "I'll give you credit for a novel story," he comments, motioning for you to be taken away. "But I can tell by your accent that you're not American."

Your whole group is processed like cattle. You're labeled members of a tribe that you've never heard of and "endorsed out" to a faraway tribal "homeland." Your only consolation is that Henry is able to claim that he's your father, so at least he will be able to look after you. Unfortunately you're powerless to stop the bomb plot, and too late to save Abraham Mabaso's life.

The End

Johannes takes you to a "nonwhite" bus depot. When he drops you off, you're embarrassed to have to ask him for one last favor—a loan for bus fare. "Bandits stole my money and my passport," you explain. "I'll pay you back out of my first paycheck."

Johannes heaves another big sigh, but he hands over the money. "Pay it back when you can," he calls as he waves good-bye. "Good luck."

As you wait for a bus, you reflect on your encounter with Johannes and Evelyn. You know you're lucky they've treated you so well. It's true they did grow up with racist assumptions, but underneath they seem to be honest people. Their worst trait may be their ignorance. Maybe blacks aren't the only ones in South Africa in desperate need of education, you reason.

Willem and his cronies, though, are another matter. As you wait for a bus to pull up, you begin to wonder how you're going to stop them from carrying out their plot to kill Abraham Mabaso.

When a bus finally comes, you discover that "nonwhite" bus service is very slow and roundabout. After several stops and changes of bus, you've only made it as far as one of the "closer settlements," still four hours from the city.

Turn to page 6.

Now, as you wait at the South African border, the immigration officer finally returns. He is accompanied by a brown-haired man sporting a prim mustache and a crisp new khaki outfit. "This is Mr. Vorman, your escort," the immigration officer announces. Vorman's composure dissolves for a second as he seems to take in the racial diversity of your group.

As Mr. Vorman leads your group out to a van, he says, "We'll stop first in one of the tribal reserves—the homelands. I think you'll be impressed with the brand new elementary school we've helped to build there."

Once you're on the road, Mr. Vorman launches into a well-rehearsed speech. "We firmly believe that education is the key to the improvement of the Bantu race. Once blacks have the training and know-how, they can turn their tribal homelands into thriving economic centers."

Although his words sound good, you know that the reality is very different. Soon you see it for yourself—you know immediately when you've entered the homeland. You cross from the rolling, lush farmlands and well-paved roads of white South Africa into a country of rutted, twisting roads, sun-blasted hills, ramshackle huts, broken-down fences, and underfed cattle and goats. Most of the land has been overgrazed or is unsuitable for farming. You know from your research that well over half these people live below the minimum subsistence level, and that there are few jobs available to them.

Turn to page 5.

The bus seems to stop every twenty minutes, and it's well past dawn before you reach the outskirts of Johannesburg. Once there, you get directions and take two local buses to the area where Willem's rendezvous is to take place.

You walk uneasily through the gently curving streets of the "white" suburb. After the bustle of the black areas you've been to, there's something spooky about these huge, silent houses and their well-trimmed gardens—all protected by guard dogs, iron bars, and tall brick walls with spiked glass. The neighborhood seems like one big fortress. You sense not only luxury here, but fear.

You arrive at 34 Verhoeven just before ten o'clock. The opulence of the Dutch-style mansion makes you wonder who exactly is bankrolling this conspiracy. You also wonder how you're going to stop it. There's no time left—but there's nothing like a deadline to get your wits going. A plan comes to you in a flash of inspiration.

Turn to page 66.

Joyce leads your group on the half-mile walk into the village. In spite of all that you've read, you're still not prepared for the reality of what you see. Mud huts and tin shacks are scattered along the roads, a few fields of stunted corn planted behind them. Children in tattered shirts and patchwork clothes play in the dusty streets. A few lucky ones have tennis shoes.

The men have gone off to find jobs in the distant urban areas, so the majority of the inhabitants are women. They carry overflowing baskets or large bundles of wood on their heads and tend their gardens, trying to coax fruits and vegetables from the barren soil.

You stop at a food stand where an old woman is roasting mealies, or corn cobs, on a brazier. You start to ask for one, when a flash of something in a window across the street catches your eye. It's only a blur, but you thought you saw a creature with a red face, bare bones, and animal fur.

Glancing up the road, you see that Joyce and the group are continuing on ahead. You know you shouldn't get separated from them, but you're drawn to the window. Maybe you can investigate and catch up with the group later.

If you decide to go and look inside the window, turn to page 10.

If you decide you'd better catch up with Joyce, turn to page 85.

You leave the guest room and slip out of Roger's house without making a sound. As you're leaving, though, you notice a few rand notes—South African currency—sitting on a side table. You pocket them, leaving a note that you'll send him a check when you get home. Then you walk the streets of the town, find a bus stop, and settle down to wait.

A couple of hours later, more people gather at the stop. They're all white. As they queue up, they stare at you.

A long-distance bus finally arrives, but the driver won't let you get on. Without a word, he points to the sign printed on the bench: NET BLANKES/ WHITES ONLY. You had been sitting with your back against the sign.

"Where can *I* get a bus?" you ask the driver.

"Eight kilometers," he says, waving vaguely to the east.

Turn to page 93.

Lunch is cut short when Lambert's beeper calls him to other business, but he promises to resume your discussion tomorrow. That afternoon, you start to hear reports that the confrontation between student protesters and the police in Soweto has turned violent. Apparently a handful of students threw rocks at the police, who were armed with teargas, whips, rifles, and shotguns. After a few warning shots, the police opened fire on the crowd, killing several children.

According to rumor, rioting has followed throughout the township. Police cars are being overturned and set alight, windows smashed, and shops looted. The authorities have sealed off the black township and are dropping teargas from helicopters on mobs of angry students. A pall of smoke from countless fires drifts over the ridge separating Soweto from Johannesburg.

Turn to page 52.

You're starting to wonder if you've made a terrible mistake, but you plunge ahead. "Not all the police agree with you, you know," you say. "I'll give you an option, though. You can go scot-free."

"What are you talking about?" Willem demands, doubt creeping into his voice.

"What I'm talking about is this—you leave your guns and your bomb where they are and get out of here right now," you say. "I tell the police it was a false tip, and keep the weapons myself."

Hendrik snarls, "I'd rather die than leave our weapons to this—"

"This is your only choice," you say, cutting him off. "You have about thirty seconds."

The four men laugh, but you can tell they're nervous. Then a knock comes at the door. "Open up!" a voice commands in Afrikaans. "Police!"

"I don't recognize the voice," Willem says to his coconspirators in a panicked tone. "Quick, let's get out of here!"

Willem grabs the gun out of Hendrik's hand and throws it to the other side of the room. The four men pile out the back door. You lock it behind them, then open the front door. The gardener is standing there with his rake.

"Did it work?" he asks.

"You were great," you reply. "They're scrambling over the back fence as we speak."

"Good," he says, shaking his fist in that direction. "I just wish I could have gotten my hands on them myself."

The End

66

Just then a black man in overalls opens the iron gate to the driveway. Judging from his tools, he must be a gardener. You run over to him and describe Willem's car.

"I haven't seen it," he shrugs. Then, arching his eyebrows and looking over his shoulder, he adds, "Until right now."

You freeze for a moment, then pick up a rake. Keeping your back to the driveway, you pretend you're working. The gardener waves to Willem and the men inside the car.

Once the car has gone up the driveway, you quickly explain that the men inside are planning to kill Abraham Mabaso. "But I've got a plan to stop them. Will you help me?" you ask the gardener.

He looks doubtful but agrees. "Great," you say. "How's your Afrikaans?"

Turn to page 8.

The girl's name is Mary. As she tells you more about the witch doctor, you notice she's adorned with traditional beads and bracelets, but at the same time is wearing leg warmers and running shoes.

You're so absorbed in what Mary is saying that you completely lose track of time—not to mention Joyce! As you realize this, you snap your notebook shut. "Thank you very much," you say quickly. "I've got to run."

"You're welcome," Mary says. As you leave, you turn around in time to see her hoist an enormous container of water onto her head and walk away, her hands at her sides.

You dash off in the direction your companions were going, but quickly realize there's no way to catch up with them. Your only hope is to go back to the elementary school where the van is parked.

You turn around and go sprinting through the village. People stare after you. You look for the school, but you're disoriented—you can't remember the direction you came from. There are no signs, the roads curve all over the place, and there are few landmarks to help you.

You stop, exhausted and panting, and realize you have no idea where you are. You grab people passing by and frantically ask if they've seen any foreigners or if they know where the school is. Everyone just shakes their heads.

Finally, wandering around hopelessly, you spy the school down at the bottom of the hill. Unfortunately the van, and your friends, are long gone.

Turn to page 13.

"All right," you say to Roger, "let's go to Soweto."

"It's always best to be the defender rather than the aggressor," he says, putting the car in gear and easing back onto the road.

The first light of day begins to show before you finally come over the ridge that separates modern white Johannesburg from Soweto, the isolated living area, or "township" for blacks. The smooth multilane avenues give way to rutted, two-lane streets. Traffic crawls along through regimented matchbox houses. Hardly anything green is growing, the ground is hard, and a pall of smoke from cooking fires hangs over the township. Soweto, you know from your research, still has not been modernized with electricity.

Soweto seems to go on forever, block after block of bleak asbestos-roofed houses, or in some places, squatter's shanties. You reach a commercial intersection with a few operating businesses. Roger seems nervous. "Perhaps you'd better do the talking," he says.

Turn to page 45.

The procession is fairly orderly at first, but soon it is overtaken by disturbances continued from the previous day's killings.

As the procession turns onto a larger street, you and Mbuto run into a scene of total chaos. Buildings and overturned school buses are burning. Helicopters hover overhead, bombing the area with teargas. Police wearing gas masks are trying to beat back an angry mob of demonstrators with truncheons, whips, and rubber bullets. Armored police cars are pelted with stones and bottles as they make periodic runs at the crowd, trying to break it up. Policemen with shotguns, rifles, and whips roam the side streets.

Mbuto hands you a handkerchief to hold over your mouth. Coughing and choking from the smoke and teargas, he grabs your hand and manages to lead you to safety back at the house.

"I've never seen anything like this," Mbuto says to you. "Never have people vented their anger in such fashion—not in my generation, at least. The young people now are different. They've seen their parents and grandparents try to bring about change, and things have only gotten worse. The racist government has armed itself to the teeth and come up with new ways to control and repress us. Those students out there feel they have nothing to lose."

Turn to page 97.

"Okay, Mbuto, let's do it," you say, a surge of adrenaline pumping through your body. "But how are we going to break out?"

"A lot depends on you getting your passport back," Mbuto replies. "Or at least on your convincing them that you are who you say you are."

You and Mbuto stay up late into the night, hatching a plan. In the morning, you're hauled out of your cell to see the police captain who waves your passport in front of your face.

"We found this in the car that was confiscated last night," he informs you. "Your companions are backing up your story. However, you have some serious visa problems."

"Speaking of problems," you interrupt, "why did you put me in with a terrorist?"

The captain stops. Folding his arms with interest, he says, "A terrorist?"

"Of course!" you go on. "The man is a member of the A.N.C. He couldn't stop blabbing about all his infiltration missions. He even told me where he left some secret documents in the bush!"

The captain stands up. "Take us there."

"I don't know the exact location. We'd have to bring him along," you say, jerking your head back toward the cell.

The captain nods swiftly at the two guards in the room. Soon you're outside, in the backseat of a land rover, waiting for Mbuto to be brought out.

"Traitor!" Mbuto spits as he is pushed into a vehicle behind you, his eyes narrow with hate. So far everything is going according to plan.

Turn to page 34.

You're surprised by the neutral tone in which Henry tells his story. Somehow he has kept himself from becoming bitter over the way he and his family have been treated by the apartheid regime.

You proceed to tell Henry how you've come to be where you are, including the bomb plot set for tomorrow.

"We've got to save Abraham Mabaso!" Henry says.

"I know, but how?" you reply.

"We'll take the train," Henry declares after some thought.

"How can we get on the train? You said you have no money, and I've been robbed. I don't even have my passport anymore," you remind him.

"We don't get on the train, we get on *top* of the train," Henry says with a smile.

You look at him in disbelief. "Haven't you heard of staffriding?" he asks.

Staffriding, you discover, is the daredevil practice of riding illegally on top of railway cars.

You're unsure you want to try this risky maneuver. "Isn't there another way?" you ask Henry.

"Probably," he shrugs. "But this is the only way I can guarantee we'll get to the city by tomorrow morning. It's up to you."

If you decide to try staffriding, turn to page 28.

If you tell Henry you want to find another way, turn to page 42.

"I'm of Trinidadian–Irish descent," you say tersely. "Now let me go."

Sergeant Frikkie throws up his hands. "We have no choice. Can't hold a colored for not having a passbook." He stands up and shows you to the door. "Just remember, next time you come in here making up stories, I'll have you put in solitary confinement on Robben Island." He's not smiling.

You feel humiliated. You thought you could rise above the system of racism and apartheid here, but it has forced you to submit. As you reflect, you realize that you're lucky in one respect. The people who live here must face these choices every day.

You turn around to leave, but stop abruptly as you reach the door. Suddenly you realize that with no one to help you, your chances of stopping the bomb plot will be slim. Once again you must humble yourself before the sergeant. "Is there a minister in town I could speak with?" you ask, hoping Frikkie considers himself a religious man.

The sergeant chuckles. "Yeah, I guess so. English liberal, he is. Name's Roger. He likes your kind."

Turn to page 81.

You feel a sense of exhilaration once you decide to explore South Africa on your own. But you know it will not be easy. For one thing, your skin is the wrong color, at least as far as most white South Africans are concerned. Your mother is Irish, but your father grew up on the island of Trinidad and has jet-black skin. You've inherited his Caribbean accent as well, so people don't always know that you're an American.

Growing up in New York, you were certainly acquainted with racism more than once. But, after the civil rights movement of the 1960s, you've been lucky enough to live in a good neighborhood and go to schools where you've been able to do most of the things you've wanted.

Under South Africa's system of apartheid, more than half the blacks in South Africa have been stripped of their citizenship and declared citizens of their "homeland." They must carry passbooks, which outline where they are allowed to travel. Blacks in South Africa find these Pass Laws humiliating. A policeman can demand to see their passbooks at any time. If they do not have one, or if it's not stamped for the area they are in, they can be thrown in jail.

Go on to the next page.

While it can be very difficult for blacks to travel in South Africa, you think you should have no problem as long as you have your American passport. Before you go anywhere, though, you need to find a place to sleep for the night.

You walk back into the village, the sun sinking red on the horizon behind you. Now luck is on your side. You find someone who can give you directions to Mary's house. You knock at her door, and after you tell her what has happened, she insists that you stay at her house for the night.

Turn to page 19.

"I'm not going to be classified by any of your categories!" you scream defiantly.

Sergeant Frikkie snaps his fingers and commands again, "Passbook."

"I don't have one," you say calmly.

"Then you're in big trouble," he hisses. "All blacks are supposed to carry passbooks. You're under arrest."

Suddenly you realize that if you're detained, you won't be able to stop the assassination plot. "Wait a minute," you say as the sergeant sits back down to fill out the papers. "I was robbed. My passport was stolen. I'm really an American."

The sergeant doesn't look up.

"Ask me about the States—baseball, New York, anything," you plead.

"Never been there," Frikkie replies. "I wouldn't know if you're lying, any more than you've been lying from the moment you walked in here."

You give in. "I'm allowed one phone call, aren't I?" you ask, hoping it's the same as it is back home.

"No," he snaps. "But since no one can help you anyway, I suppose I'll let you use our telephone."

Your mind is racing as you dial the operator in Pretoria. You manage to get through to Jack Lambert's company and leave a message for him. "Please tell him it's an emergency. I'm being held by the police in—"

Frikkie murmurs the name of the town. You repeat it into the telephone. "Mr. Lambert and my adviser, Joyce Jenkins, are meeting with a minister in the Department of Education this morning."

Turn to page 115.

You decide that in order to save Abraham Mabaso, you'll have to take positive action. You jump up, march into the minister's room, and shake him awake. He sits up with a fright.

You turn on the light and tell him to get dressed. "We don't have much time. We've got to do something now."

Roger puts on his glasses and squints at you. "But what?" he fusses. "We're just two—"

"I think I can find the farmhouse where they're making the bomb," you say. "Let's go now. We'll figure out what to do once we get there."

Minutes later you are speeding down a dark country highway. You wander around for a while, but finally you recognize the road leading to the abandoned farmhouse. "The driveway is just down here," you say. "We're almost there."

Roger abruptly pulls over on the shoulder. "I don't know if this is a good idea," he says. "These fellows are dangerous. I really don't think we should confront them ourselves. Let's call the police."

"No police," you say firmly.

Go on to the next page.

"Well then, let's go find Abraham Mabaso and warn him," Roger suggests.

"That means driving all the way to Soweto," you point out.

"We've got all night," Roger replies. "If we do it your way, all that's likely to happen is we'll get ourselves killed and save nobody."

You take a moment to consider. Maybe Roger is right. Maybe the smarter and safer course of action is to try and track down the antiapartheid leader in Soweto. Soweto, however, contains two million people. He may be hard to find.

If you decide to go to the farmhouse, turn to page 91.

If you decide to go to Soweto, turn to page 68.

Mr. Lambert sits back and sighs. "All of your arguments are good ones," he says, and then tries to convince you that it is better for his company to be here than not. He goes on to describe how the company has adopted fair employment practices, started a program to train black managers, and set up a fund to improve education for blacks.

"All of these are commendable," Joyce says when he's finished. "But they're just not enough. They're only drops in the bucket when the bucket needs to be kicked over. The basic situation must change. And I have to tell you, until it does, I will continue to campaign for American companies to stop investing money in South Africa."

"But that helps no one," Lambert objects, looking hurt by her words. "The unemployment rate among blacks is already tremendously high, and this will only make it worse. If we pull out, we'll be replaced by other, less responsible investors."

"It will put pressure on the government to make real changes," Joyce counters. "The A.N.C. is calling for foreign investors to pull out, and that's good enough for me."

As you listen to Joyce and Mr. Lambert debate, you try to make sense of it all. The basic problem in South Africa seems very simple, yet the more you learn, the more complicated the solutions seem. You'll certainly have a lot to think about, and a lot to write about, when you return to New York.

The End

Frikkie, surprisingly, calls one of his men to give you a ride to the minister's house. You leave the station and approach the front door of the squad car. "In the back," the policeman tells you.

He drops you off at a small house next to a modest brick church. "Watch out for terrorists!" the policeman says sarcastically as you get out.

You ring the doorbell. A middle-aged man in a clerical collar answers. Peering at you from behind thick spectacles, he says, "May I help you?"

"Yes," you say, stepping inside. You introduce yourself, then walk into the living room and start right in with your story. As you talk, you see that Roger is a portly man with watery eyes and carefully manicured fingernails.

Turn to page 14.

Deciding to go to the police, you wait until the car has driven off, then circle around a barn behind the house and cut across the veld to the road.

You jump up and down and wave frantically at the first car that comes along. It stops, but the white couple inside seems uncomfortable talking to you. Once you explain that you want a ride to the nearest police station, they become less fearful.

An hour later you are in a farm town, pounding on the door of a small police station. A strapping blond police sergeant with a brush cut answers. He looks you over. "Well?" he says with a sneer.

"I have important information about a terrorist plot," you say warily.

His eyes light up. "Do come in," he says, suddenly polite. He brings you into a small office where two other similar-looking policemen are laughing. They stop when they see you.

The sergeant goes behind his desk and gestures for you to sit in a wooden chair in the middle of the room. "Talk," he says.

You glance at the other two officers who stand on either side of you, thumbs hooked in their belts. You take a breath and relate what you overheard in the abandoned farmhouse.

"Hold on," the sergeant interrupts. "These men you're describing—they're white?"

"Well, yes," you reply, startled.

"These men are Afrikaner nationalists protecting their homes," he shoots back. "It's Mabaso who is the terrorist."

Turn to page 99.

"I once worked in those government buildings as a janitor," Henry says as you hurry to keep up. "I know a way to get inside."

"Really?" you say, impressed. "You can sneak us into the Department of Education?"

"No problem," Henry replies. "You know, the government thinks we cannot run this country, but it's we blacks who do all the work. We know their cities better than they do."

Your first stop is a tin shack near the railyard where a friend of Henry's lives. From him you each borrow a pair of blue overalls, the typical outfit of a laborer. Henry also manages to borrow a little money from his friend. With a combination of bus rides and jogging, you make it to the Department of Education before nine o'clock.

Henry takes you around to the back entrance of the building. As you arrive, the trash is being collected. You and Henry help out for a couple of minutes, then slip into the building. Another worker in blue overalls recognizes Henry and greets him. "I didn't know you were working here again," he says.

"Just started today," Henry says cheerfully. "Do you know where we can get a couple of push brooms?"

The worker takes you to a closet on the same floor as Joyce's meeting with the minister.

Turn to page 30.

You run to catch up with Joyce and the group, the strange image you glimpsed through the window still haunting you. As you wander around the village, you wonder if you'll ever find out what it was.

Before you know it, Joyce announces that it's time to return to the school parking lot. Your group protests, but she overrules. "Mr. Vorman is waiting to take us to the station," she reminds you. It's the last train to Pretoria, and we can't miss it."

It's late when the train pulls into Pretoria Station, but Jack Lambert is waiting for you as scheduled. He's a tall, good-looking man with sun-bronzed skin and an easygoing manner. He greets you warmly. "I hope your travels in South Africa have been happy so far," he says, motioning to some porters to get your group's luggage.

Lambert takes you to an "international" hotel, one that accommodates both blacks and whites. He seems eager to prove to your group that he treats everyone the same, although his effort seems a little forced.

"We've got a big meeting tomorrow morning," he says as he bids you good night. "The minister has graciously consented to give us half an hour of his time. I'll see you then."

Turn to page 26.

As the men talk, you realize that they are part of a white supremacist organization. Their plot to set off a bomb tomorrow in Soweto, the enormous collection of black townships outside of Johannesburg, is designed not only to kill Abraham Mabaso and many other innocent bystanders, but to put the blame on the African National Congress. This could trigger fighting between individual black groups, validating the government feeling that blacks are too violent to negotiate with.

You've got to prevent the plot from succeeding. But how? Normally, you'd go to the police. But in South Africa, and especially way out here in the veld, the police are not necessarily neutral enforcers of the law. Some may agree with the goals of the white supremacists. From the sound of it, Willem has sympathetic friends in high places.

Your ears prick up as Willem asks Hendrik to come to the car with him. Stephan and Osgood walk them outside. Now's your chance to slip out of the house. Silently you glide down the stairs and through the kitchen. Your timing is perfect—you make it out the back door just as Stephan and Osgood are returning though the front.

Go on to the next page.

You run along the side of the house and peer around the edge. Willem and Hendrik are already in the car. You hear the ignition turn.

It's time to make a decision. You know that going to the police is chancy. Your only other choice is to follow Willem and Hendrik and try to come up with a way to stop them, which is just as risky. Whatever you're going to do, you'd better hurry. The car is pulling out.

If you decide to go to the police,
turn to page 82.

If you decide to follow the men in the car,
turn to page 37.

You make it to Johannesburg that evening and from there catch a bus to Soweto. When you arrive, you get some idea of what Mbuto is talking about. You're struck by how gray and grim the area is, worse even than you had imagined. Burnt-out cars and buildings dot the landscape. A pall of gray smoke obscures the setting sun.

"Something's going on," Mbuto comments. "There's always an evening haze in Soweto—without electricity, people cook over fires. But this is much worse than usual."

Mbuto brings you to a "safe house" for freedom fighters. There you hear the news: the confrontation between police and student demonstrators heated up today, and the police fired on the crowd, killing several children. The township immediately exploded in violence. There have been riots, looting, more police shootings, and rumors of police informers being murdered.

You can see that Mbuto is barely able to control his anger and sadness. Nevertheless, he asks if you want to attend a funeral procession for a fallen comrade tomorrow. He warns you that it could be very dangerous. With other kinds of political expression outlawed, funerals have become occasions for protest. You're scared, but you tell him you'd like to go.

You accompany Mbuto to the funeral procession the next morning. A throng of mourners, at once grieving and protesting, surrounds the casket. A chant of *"Amandla! Awethu!"* begins. Mbuto tells you the words mean "Power is ours!"

Turn to page 69.

"Evelyn!" the Boer calls as he scrapes the mud off his boots in the entryway. "We've got a foreign guest for lunch."

"All right, Johannes," his wife calls back. As she enters the room she looks a little taken aback when she sees you. As she prepares the midday meal, you can't help but notice that the dishes she takes for you come from a separate cupboard than the ones she uses for her husband.

During the course of your meal, you manage to get your hosts talking about South Africa. They have no problem stating their views frankly. "This country must be ruled by whites," Johannes declares, surprising you with his straightforward prejudice. "It may be different where you come from, but blacks here simply don't have the necessary skills or the knack for running things. No offense, you understand, but some people are better at some things than others."

Turn to page 9.

"I think we should go to the farmhouse," you tell Roger. "But I'll tell you what. We'll wait until after midnight. If we're lucky, they'll be asleep. We'll sneak inside then and steal the bomb."

"This is foodhardy," Roger mutters, but he doesn't argue any further. You wait in the car, drifting in and out of sleep. All of a sudden Roger is shaking you. "It's past midnight," he says, starting the engine.

By the time you reach the driveway to the farmhouse, you're wide awake. Roger turns off his lights and coasts down to the house. No lights come on from inside.

Slowly the two of you creep up to the porch. The front lock is still broken from your previous entry. You push the door open cautiously and step inside.

The house is completely silent and dark. You move slowly, taking a step and then stopping for two breaths, taking another step and stopping. As you come into the living room, your eyes adjust to the darkness. You notice an object on top of a table—the bomb. As you take another step, a floorboard lets out a hideous creak.

You freeze and look back at Roger in horror. For a long second all is quiet. Then, from the kitchen, the mad barking of a dog rips through the house.

Turn to page 33.

Mr. Lambert takes you and your group to lunch at an Indian restaurant. As you wait for your order to come, Joyce asks him what he means when he says his company is in favor of reform.

"You talk of it all the time, yet nothing seems to change," she says. "Don't companies like yours benefit from apartheid in the long run? You cloak yourselves in pleasant words and good intentions, yet somehow you manage to live with the fact that real change hardly ever happens."

"But Ms. Jenkins, we don't benefit in the long run," Lambert objects. "This place is a tinderbox. It could explode at any time. Obviously, it is in our interest to have a peaceful transition to equal rights for blacks, rather than chaos."

"True," Joyce says, "but when will you stop exploiting them?"

Lambert seems pained. "We don't exploit them," he says. "We give them jobs. We even have managers who are black."

Turn to page 63.

Angry and dejected, you walk out to the highway. You put out your thumb, but no one stops. Finally, while you're jumping up and down to keep warm, a black truck driver pulls over.

"Where are you headed?" he asks.

"I've got to get to Johannesburg," you reply, reminding yourself of the location of Willem's rendezvous.

"I can get you close."

"Sounds good," you answer with a shiver.

The driver drops you off at a station where, he says, you'll be able to get a bus to one of the "closer settlements," or black-only areas near the cities. You thank him, and soon after he leaves, a bus arrives.

Turn to page 6.

94

Wearily you get back to your feet. After stumbling through a field of withered cornstalks, you suddenly come across a farmhouse. Cautiously you circle it. It seems to be abandoned. You throw your body against the door and crash inside. You can't see a thing, but you manage to bump your way into the kitchen. You find a knife in one of the drawers and wedge it into a position where you are able to cut the ropes free from your hands.

An enormous exhaustion overtakes you. You feel your way over to a staircase and climb up to a room where an old mattress lies on the floor. You collapse into a deep sleep.

Turn to page 41.

Your mission is more important than any sign. You open the door of the restaurant, step in, and survey the dining room.

Willem and Hendrik are taking a booth near the back. The rest of the dining room seems to be occupied by beefy Boers—Afrikaner farmers—and truck drivers. Not exactly a sympathetic crowd, you think to yourself. Still, they wouldn't want Willem to carry out his plot to assassinate Abraham Mabaso, would they?

A waitress approaches you looking annoyed. Before she can say anything, you gesture toward Willem's booth. "Do you know those two men?" you whisper to her. "They're terrorists. They're on their way to plant a bomb in Soweto."

Turn to page 100.

Your eyes are still stinging from the smoke and teargas, and you continue to gasp for breath. Before you can respond, Mbuto goes on, "It is dangerous here. This may be the end, or the beginning—the whole country may explode." You think you detect both excitement and apprehension in his voice. "You are welcome to stay on as my guest, but I think it might be better for you to try to join up with your group. Besides, you never know when the police might catch up with us."

You agree. According to your itinerary, your group is already in Cape Town. If you want to catch them in time to make your flight back to New York, you should leave now.

You and Mbuto manage to find a public telephone that's still working, and you call Jack Lambert. He's relieved to hear from you. "I was terribly worried," he says. "It's too bad we won't have a chance to meet, but right now I think the important thing is to get you to Cape Town. If you can make it to Johannesburg, I'll have someone waiting there for you with papers and a ticket."

You thank Mr. Lambert for his help and turn to Mbuto. "I guess this is good-bye," you say. "Thank you for everything you've done for me."

"You've been helpful to me as well," Mbuto reminds you. "I hope you will write about what you've seen when you return to the United States. The world needs to know."

You give him your word that you will.

The End

"Let's ditch the land rover," you say to Mbuto. "Sooner or later it'll give us away."

Mbuto drives for a while, then pulls off the road into a clump of high bushes. You cover up the vehicle as best you can. Then you and Mbuto set off on foot. You're near the homeland where Mbuto thinks he might have some relatives.

You go up and down over rugged, close-set hills. Much of the land is eroded, leaving only hard, gray clay. You drop down into dry, washed-out gullies, then pass by *kraals,* or cattle enclosures, as you climb over the tops of the hills.

You're climbing up the side of a hill when you see a group of four men armed with rifles at the top. Mbuto stops dead in his tracks. "Cattle rustlers," he murmurs.

The men have spotted you. One of them comes ahead and asks Mbuto questions in a language you don't understand. Once they start talking, you gather that he and Mbuto are going through an elaborate greeting ritual. Mbuto later explains to you that they were telling each other the names of their fathers, grandfathers, and great-grand-fathers; the name of the river their clan drinks from; and how their herds are faring.

You see Mbuto's expression relax. He exchanges farewells with the man and gestures to you to continue walking up the hill. "He told me that we'll find a family related to mine over the second hill."

Turn to page 16.

"No, you don't understand," you insist. "I heard it myself, not two hours ago. These guys are right-wing extremists. They're going to set off a bomb in Soweto!"

"You're wasting my time," the sergeant declares with disgust. "I thought you were talking about *real* terrorists."

"They *are* real terrorists!" you protest. "You've got to stop them."

"Listen, we can't investigate every rumor of assassination plots," he says, shaking his head back and forth. The other two policemen nod in agreement. "That's right, Frikkie," one of them says.

"But this is no rumor!" you burst out.

The sergeant appraises you with a look of cold superiority. "Why should we believe some *kaffir* kid?"

You nearly leap out of your chair. *Kaffir* is the derogatory term whites use for black Africans. Your face burns with anger and humiliation. "Listen, Sergeant Frikkie, I'm not a *kaffir!*" you scream in frustration.

Frikkie stands up, towering over you. His lips are pressed in a grim line. "My friends call me Sergeant Frikkie," he says. "You call me *baas.*" *Baas,* meaning "boss," is the word blacks are often expected to use when addressing whites.

Frikkie sits back down and puts his fingertips together. "Now, since when are you not a *kaffir?*"

"No one is a *kaffir,*" you say angrily. "It's a demeaning word that applies to no one."

Turn to page 46.

The waitress bursts into laughter. "Willem and Hendrik?" she says in a loud voice. "They're two of my best customers."

"You've got to help me stop them," you insist. "Call the police, do something—"

"Listen, you'd better stop bad-mouthing my friends," she says, turning nasty.

Things are going badly. A nearby table of Boers is eyeing you suspiciously. Willem and Hendrik may have already overheard your exchange. Perhaps you should confront them loudly and clearly, hoping they'll give themselves away and the other patrons will help you out.

Then again, maybe you should leave right now, while you still have a chance. You have about three seconds to decide, because two of the Boers have stood up and are lumbering your way.

If you confront Willem and Hendrik right now, turn to page 38.

If you think you'd better leave, turn to page 44.

You awaken at dawn after a night on the earthen floor. Mary is already up and cooking. Breakfast is very similar to dinner. After you eat, you thank Mary for her hospitality.

"I'm sure it was not what you are used to," she says, and prepares to send you in the direction of a larger village 20 kilometers to the south. Once there you will be able to catch a bus. You're not sure exactly where you want to go, but you have the whole of South Africa in front of you. You thank Mary again and promise to send her a copy of your article when you return home.

The road south is a small dusty track winding through dry, rolling bushland. Jagged mountains rise to the east. After 20 minutes you look back and notice a puff of dust in the distance. Soon an old flatbed truck comes rattling along. The back is already jammed with people, but they hold out their hands for you to climb aboard. You cling to the outside of the railing as the truck bounces on down the road.

A few kilometers later, you approach a cluster of trees at the crest of a hill. A man standing beside the road appears to want a ride. But as the truck slows down, you spot four more men armed with guns lurking in the trees.

Go on to the next page.

"Go! They're *skollies*," you shout to the driver, remembering Vorman's word for bandits.

The driver hits the gas, and the truck lurches forward. You can barely hang on. The bandits dive out of the way as the truck screams into high gear.

You are looking back, thinking you're safe, when a tree branch catches you on the side of the head. You're thrown from the truck. The last thing you see before you pass out is the world spinning upside down.

Turn to page 20.

The idea of traveling alone in South Africa seems too scary. You need to catch up to Joyce and the rest of the group as quickly as you can.

You wander back into the village and soon discover that in order to get a bus to the train, you'll have to go to a larger village 20 kilometers to the south. You set out in that direction, wondering if you're going to have to walk the whole way. Darkness is coming, and you remember Mr. Vorman's warnings about bandits.

Half an hour later, a battered Volkswagen comes careening down the road. It's jammed with young people who look like they're going to a party. The car screeches to a stop, and someone offers you a lift.

You squeeze into the backseat, and the car swerves ahead, sometimes staying on the road, sometimes crashing through the bush. The passengers are singing songs and passing around a bottle of bootleg cane liquor, and it soon becomes clear that they're on their way to a *shebeen,* an illegal bar. You remember Joyce explaining that drinking is a problem in the homelands and townships because people's lives are so difficult.

The car lurches to a stop in the center of the village and all of you tumble out. Picking yourself up, you see a policeman coming your way. You're about to ask directions to the bus stop when you find yourself staring down the barrel of his gun.

"Nobody move! You're all under arrest for public drunkenness," the policeman announces in a booming voice.

Turn to page 24.

"They're after us!" you say, looking behind.

Mbuto keeps the land rover bouncing through the bush at breakneck speed, somehow staying on the faint dirt track. Gradually the distance between you and the homeland police increases.

Eventually you reach a paved road. As Mbuto pulls onto it, you look back. The other land rover is nowhere in sight.

"We lost them!" you say.

"That was the easy part," Mbuto replies. "It's the South African police I'm worried about. They'll have helicopters and dogs after us. Every road in the region will be blocked."

"What can we do?" you ask.

"We can try to make it farther south and then ditch the land rover," Mbuto answers. "The problem with that is then we have no money and no transportation."

"That doesn't sound very good," you say.

"I think I have some relatives in the tribal reserve there. I've never spoken to them, but if we can make it that far, maybe we could find them."

"What's our other choice?"

"We could go through the bush, cross-country, and try to make it to the border."

Neither option holds much promise. But Mbuto seems to be waiting for you to make a choice.

If you decide to ditch the land rover, turn to page 98.

If you decide to try to go cross-country to the border, turn to page 110.

With tremendous effort, you slide the bale of hay up to the edge of the flatbed and push it off.

At the moment you let it fly, Hendrik shoots out the tire of the truck. It swerves wildly. You have enough time to see the bale bounce once on the highway, then up onto Willem's hood and through the windshield.

The truck careens off the road, down the shoulder, and tips over. As you and several bales of hay go flying into the air, you see Willem's car flip over. It lands and bursts into a ball of fire.

When you hit the ground, you roll a few times and come to rest in a pile of hay. For the second time in less than an hour you pick yourself up and probe for broken bones. You've got plenty of scratches and bruises, but luckily, once again, you're okay.

You run to see if the farmer is all right. He's busy pulling himself out of the truck through his broken window, his face covered with blood. As soon as he sees you, he screams. "You again! Wait till I get my hands on you!"

The farmer doesn't appear to be too seriously injured. Once you've helped him get to his feet, you manage to calm him down while you use your kerchief to cover the wound on his head. He looks over at the burning car and grimaces. "Poor fellows. I don't suppose there's much left of them."

"Don't feel too sorry for them," you say. "They tried to kill me."

Turn to page 40.

Mbuto sighs. "There are many reasons," he says in answer to your question. "Almost everyone in this country is desperate—even just for food and shelter. Being a police officer is a job that pays. And it gives them power. For people who have been kept powerless for so long, it is very tempting. That, my friend, is the insidious thing about apartheid—it turns black against black."

"You don't hate these men?" you ask.

"I can understand their motivations," Mbuto answers. "But believe me, they are the lowest of the low—betraying their own people. I only hope that when the time comes, they'll change their minds."

You're silent for a moment, thinking about the hard choices blacks in South Africa must face every day. "Well, one thing is for sure," you say at last. "These policemen are preventing me from getting to my meeting with a minister in the Department of Education tomorrow."

Mbuto laughs heartily at your frustration. "Don't worry. Education—*real* education—is the last thing you'd get from him."

Go on to the next page.

"You're probably right," you say, laughing as well. "But tell me, do you really think change is going to come?"

"Yes," Mbuto replies emphatically. "One way or another, it will come. So much injustice cannot be done to so many people for too long. Eventually, the dam will break."

"Violently?" you ask. "Isn't there hope for a peaceful solution?"

Mbuto opens his hands. "It's not up to us," he says. "The government holds the power, and they refuse to negotiate. For many, many years, black organizations worked for change by peaceful means. The African National Congress did it for 50 years. Even Ghandi tried and failed."

Turn to page 35.

You decide to go cross-country and try to make it to the border. Mbuto swerves off the road and onto a rutted track heading east. He picks his way across the savannah, expertly maneuvering the land rover through the rough terrain.

It's not long, though, before you hear the chopping of helicopters. You keep an eye on their crisscrossing paths in the sky while Mbuto tries to steer away from them. Eventually one of them spots you and bears down on your tail.

Mbuto urges the land rover on, bouncing over rocks and fallen limbs, nearly sending you flying out of your seat. Then all of a sudden the vehicle sputters and grinds to a halt. Mbuto leans his head against the steering wheel in defeat. "We're out of gas," he moans.

Turn to page 39.

"I really wish I could go with you, Mbuto," you say. "I know I'm missing out on a rare opportunity. But I can't take the risk. I've got to join up with my group in Pretoria."

Mbuto shrugs, resigned. "Whatever's best for you. But I wouldn't count on a quick release from the police here."

Later in the evening, you discover what Mbuto meant. You're brought before the police captain, who holds up your backpack and tells you that your passport has been found. But he can't release you, he says, because you don't have a permit to visit the homeland.

"But I was part of a group," you protest. "We're meeting with a minister in the Department of Education tomorrow."

The captain raises his eyebrows, impressed. "I can give you a number to call," you go on quickly. You root through your backpack and find Jack Lambert's card. His home number is written on the back. "He can explain everything," you say, praying Mr. Lambert will be home.

It works. An hour later you're zooming down a narrow highway in a police car. You still have a chance to catch the last bus to Pretoria. You get there just in time and collapse into a seat.

The bus arrives in Pretoria late at night. The hotel where your group is staying is a short taxi ride away, and Joyce is waiting to greet you, relieved by your return. After a quick recount of your experiences, you manage to get in a couple of hours of sleep before your morning meeting.

Turn to page 26.

You collapse on a bale of hay, gasping for breath. You know you don't have time to rest, though. You've got to keep an eye on Willem's car. Climbing up on top of the bales of hay, you can see it in the distance. Silently you urge the driver of the truck on, but he doesn't seem to need it. An hour goes by, and the truck continues to keep pace with the car ahead.

You're just starting to wonder what your next step will be when you notice Willem turn on his blinker. A roadside restaurant is up ahead. Apparently he and Hendrik are going to pull over for a bite to eat. But your hay truck is not.

Your mind races. The truck is going too fast for you to jump off. The only way to make the farmer stop is to get his attention by climbing over the hay and pounding on the roof of the cab.

On the other hand, maybe you don't have to stop. You know where in Johannesburg Willem is going to rendezvous with his coconspirators, Stephan and Osgood, tomorrow morning. You could try to catch up with them there. Maybe you could even take your chances and ask the farmer to help you out. Whichever decision you choose, you have to act now. You're approaching the restaurant fast.

If you decide to jump on top of the cab, turn to page 31.

If you decide to head Willem and Hendrik off in Johannesburg, turn to page 50.

114

You study the floor for a long moment. "I guess there's not much hope," you say.

"Of course there's hope!" Mbuto bursts out. "All the government has to do is sit down at the negotiating table with us. But they won't do that until the fire gets hot enough underneath them."

"Listen," he says, "forget about your meeting tomorrow with the minister in the Department of Education. Do you *really* want a learning experience?"

You can tell Mbuto is about to make you a serious offer. "Sure," you say, even though you're not sure at all.

"Help me break out of here," he says. "We'll escape together, and I'll introduce you to my comrades in Soweto."

"Is that where you were going?"

Mbuto nods. "I have important messages from the exiled command. I was arrested not long after I'd slipped over the border."

"But how can we—I mean, we're in maximum security."

"Yes, but each has tools to help the other. Together we can escape."

You think it over for a moment. It sounds terribly risky. If you're caught, you'll be in even more trouble than you are now. As it is, you figure that with a couple of phone calls, you should be free by tomorrow. On the other hand, you may never have another opportunity to take action like this.

If you decide to take Mbuto up on his offer, turn to page 70.

If you tell him you can't, turn to page 111.

Sergeant Frikkie and the policemen make no comment about your phone conversation. They just clap you in manacles and take you to a bare cell with no windows.

The order for your release does not come until late the next day. The sergeant doesn't look at you as he unlocks your cell door and says, "You can go."

As he fills out the papers for your release, Frikkie hands you a ticket. "I'm supposed to give you this," he says tonelessly. "It's for the train to Pretoria."

It takes you the rest of the day to get to Pretoria. By the time you reach the lobby of the hotel where Joyce and your group are staying, you've heard the news—a bomb exploded in Soweto this afternoon, killing Abraham Mabaso and six others.

"If only I hadn't reacted so emotionally to the policemen," you lament after you tell Joyce your story. "I wouldn't have gotten locked up and I could have stopped the bomb from going off!"

Joyce tries to console you. "You can't go blaming yourself. Who knows if you would have been able to stop them? You might have gotten killed."

"At least I might have been able to find someone who could stop it," you moan.

"I guess we've all learned something," Joyce says. "There is a time for defiance—always. But sometimes we have to look at the bigger picture and swallow our pride. Sometimes the larger cause is more important than our personal honor."

You nod, but you still don't feel any better.

The End

ABOUT THE AUTHOR

JAY LEIBOLD was born in Denver, Colorado. He is the author of many books in the Choose Your Own Adventure series, including *Secret of the Ninja*, the sequel *Return of the Ninja*, *You Are A Millionaire*, and *Revenge of the Russian Ghost*. He lives in San Francisco.

ABOUT THE ILLUSTRATOR

LESLIE MORRILL is a designer and illustrator whose work has won him numerous awards. He has illustrated over thirty books for children, including the Bantam Classic edition of *The Wind in the Willows*. Mr. Morrill has illustrated many books in the Skylark Choose Your Own Adventure series, including *Home in Time for Christmas*, *You See the Future*, *Stranded!*, and *You Can Make A Difference*. He has also illustrated *The First Olympics*, *Mystery of the Sacred Stones*, *The Perfect Planet*, *Hurricane!*, *Inca Gold*, *Stock Car Champion*, *Alien, Go Home!*, *Grave Robbers*, and *The Treasure of the Onyx Dragon* in the Choose Your Own Adventure series. Mr. Morrill also illustrated both Super Adventure books, *Journey to the Year 3000* and *Danger Zones*.